My Secret Sunrise

My Secret Sunrise

Story and Pictures by Jasper Tomkins

GREEN TIGER PRESS
Published by Simon & Schuster
New York London Toronto Sydney Tokyo Singapore

GREEN TIGER PRESS
Simon & Schuster Building, Rockefeller Center, 1230 Avenue of the Americas,
New York, New York 10020.
Copyright © 1989 by Jasper Tomkins.
All rights reserved including the right of reproduction in whole or in part in any form.
GREEN TIGER PRESS is an imprint of Simon & Schuster.
Manufactured in Hong Kong
10 9 8 7 6 5 4 3 2
(pbk) 10 9 8 7 6 5 4 3 2
ISBN 0-671-74975-7   ISBN 0-671-74978-1 (pbk)

For the light.

The sunrise begins
when I am still asleep.

As the earth awakens,
so do I.

I dress in the cold,
and crawl quietly out
the window, because
the house is still sleeping.

I know just where
I will go.

The colors are getting
brighter and brighter.

The only sound is
the sky flowing
around my ears.

I watch out for worms
that might be
crossing the path.

The trees are smiling
as they wait for
the sun.

The birds and the frogs
are blinking.

The spider webs
are dripping.

My clothes are getting wet,
but my warm friend
is coming soon
to dry them.

I'm just in time for
the wonderful event.

"Hello sun! I've been
waiting for you."
Now I'll watch the
world come to life.

The cows, the birds,
and the bugs sing out
their joyous songs.

The clouds dance
higher and higher
to make lots of room
for the light.

The ants pour out
of their underground darkness
to greet the day.

Baby bears yawn
and rub their eyes.
Now it is time to play.

The rocks slide their
smiles around to
face the warm sun.

Dragonflies and butterflies
trace their happy patterns
in the sky.

The flowers yawn
to catch the sun.
Now they will follow it
across the sky.

The trees are admiring
their brand new,
long shadows.

The fish jump through the air
to salute the sun.

This moment
will last
forever.

I have a secret breakfast,

and ride my bike
back home.

I've seen the secret sunrise
and now it is my day.